Ama is a girl who is different from you and me.

She is friends with animals on
land and in the sea.

Nearly every day, she dives
with a dolphin called Brave
to explore the brilliant colours
underneath the waves.

The currents glow in blue,
red, silver, and green.
It is the most spectacular
beauty Ama has ever seen.

Colourful coral reefs build
cities of the sea,
where so many animals
swim, happy and free.

A sea turtle is the first friend they seek,
and very soon they sneak a peek.

He's slowly gliding along a rock cave,
and when he sees them, he gives them a wave.

Mr. Sea Turtle is so much fun. They often have a race
or play hide-and-seek, which leads to a chase.

"It is getting harder to hide," they hear him shout.
"For me, caves in coral reefs is what it's all about."

They can see that Mr. Sea Turtle is right.
It used to be easier to find spots to hide.

It is time to say goodbye, and they all agree:

**"We have to work together
to save the cities of the sea!"**

Searching for their octopus friend is the next thing they do.
But where is she? They have no clue!

Brave tells Ama something not very well known:

"An octopus has three hearts,
nine brains, but not a single bone!

That means she can fit through the tiniest space.
It is easy for her to hide in a tiny coral cave."

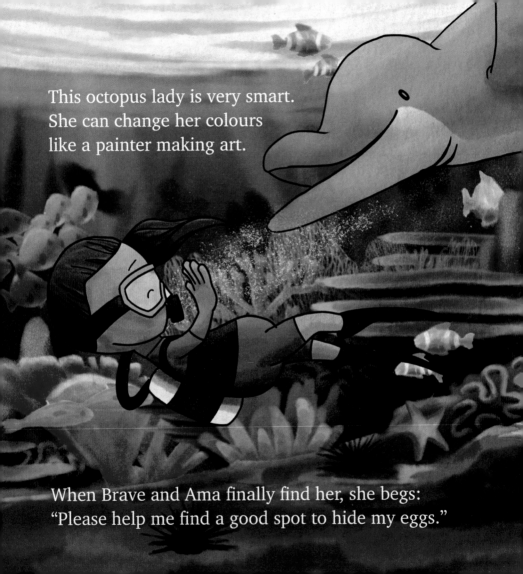

This octopus lady is very smart.
She can change her colours
like a painter making art.

When Brave and Ama finally find her, she begs:
"Please help me find a good spot to hide my eggs."

After a few hours of searching, Brave and Ama find a perfect cave for the eggs and octopus mama.

It is time to say goodbye, and they all agree:

"We have to work together to save the cities of the sea!"

After all the fun, the day soon comes to an end.
But there is time to meet one more special friend.

Ama and Brave see the colours from afar:
The bright and intense shades of a sea star.

They see so many starfish everywhere,
but then Brave calls: "He's right there!"

Mr. Starfish says: "Long time no see!
I was wondering if you could help me?"

I am hungry and have to regrow an arm,
but I don't want to do these baby corals any harm."

Eating coral makes him feel really sad.
He wants to protect the reefs, just like his mom and dad.

Of course, his two friends
help him find a treat,
and very soon Mr. Starfish
has something to eat.

It is time to say goodbye,
and they all agree:

"We have to work together to save the cities of the sea!"

Ama knows that her friends face one common fear:
Their coral reef homes slowly disappear.

The temperatures in our oceans rise,
and it is getting harder for corals to survive.

When they get sick, it is called "bleach".
Their recovery is the goal Ama wants to reach.

Ama is done
diving for the day,
but, of course,
Brave has to stay.

Before they say goodbye,
they make a plan
to help their friends
the best they can.

At her school, Ama explains how important coral is for the sea,

but also for the balance of the entire planet: for you and me.

Corals do so much, like producing air for all of us, and protecting shorelines from big waves and floods.

There are TV shows that the kids have already seen, teaching them how to help corals, even when choosing sunscreen.

FRIENDLY SCREEN

They know that corals can grow in a saltwater pool, so decide to build one with their teachers at school.

Ama, her teachers, and friends all agree:

**"We have to work together
to save the cities of the sea!"**

Brave is an important member of the team.
She can do something you have never seen!

With her melonhead, this dolphin can read echoes
to locate and identify things wherever she goes.

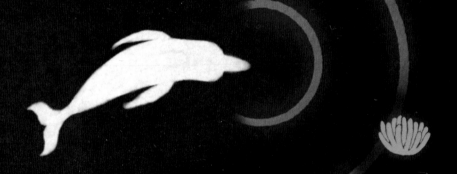

This way, she finds pieces of coral
with chances to survive
and for Ama to put in their
saltwater pool to help them thrive.

Once the corals are as strong and well as they can be,
Ama puts them on rocks to grow new reefs in the sea.

A few years later, four days after a full moon,
Ama and Brave meet by the reef in the afternoon.

But today is different, and they are full of hope
as they see the waters swirl like a snowglobe.

The team waits on the
beach by a big palm tree

while whales in the background
sing their song of the sea.

Ama hurries to tell the good
news to her friends:

"The corals are growing,
and this is not how it ends!"

They are so very
happy and all agree:

**"We will keep working to
save the cities of the sea!"**

Made in the USA
Las Vegas, NV
07 July 2021

25995783R00024